ticklish

This book belongs to

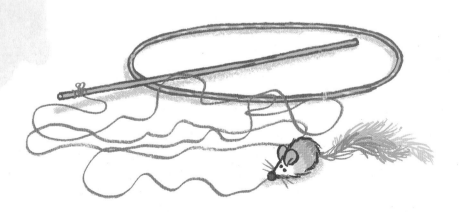

OXFORD
UNIVERSITY PRESS

Great Clarendon Street, Oxford OX2 6DP
Oxford University Press is a department of the University of Oxford.
It furthers the University's objective of excellence in research, scholarship,
and education by publishing worldwide. Oxford is a registered trade mark of
Oxford University Press in the UK and in certain other countries

Text and illustrations copyright © Richard Byrne 2018

The moral rights of the author/illustrator have been asserted
Database right Oxford University Press (maker)

First published in 2018

First published in paperback in 2019

British Library Cataloguing in Publication Data
Data available

ISBN: 978-0-19-276713-4 (paperback)

10 9 8 7 6 5 4 3 2 1
Printed in China

Paper used in the production of this book is a natural,
recyclable product made from wood grown in sustainable forests.
The manufacturing process conforms to the environmental
regulations of the country of origin.

Visit www.richardbyrne.co.uk

This book just stole my cat!

Richard BYRNE

OXFORD
UNIVERSITY PRESS

Ben and his cat were playing tickle and chase across the page when . . .

. . . something very odd happened.

Ben's cat disappeared!

'Hello Ben. You look like you've lost something!' said Bella.

'I've seen things go missing
in here before,' said Bella.
'I'll take a peek.'

But Bella disappeared too.

Help quickly arrived to begin a search and rescue mission . . .

. . . then vanished.

The search wasn't going very well at all.

'I'll just have to do the rescuing myself!' thought Ben.

But . . .

ACHOO!

Now everybody (except for a book-tickling fluffy mouse) was missing!

A little while later a message appeared.

It read . . .

Dear reader,
Please can you help rescue us?
This book seems to sneeze when
it's tickled so here are some
instruckshuns for you.

1. Wiggle your tickling fingers
to get them all warmed up.

2. TICKLE the
book in here...

...while counting tickly-one,
tickly-two. tickly-three!

3. Then turn over the page...

Everybody was rescued . . .

. . . and everything got back to normal.
(Well, almost everything!)

WHIRL
WHIRL